CHICKENS TO THE RESCUE

John Himmelman

Henry Holt and Company

New York

Henry Holt and Company, LLC
Publishers since 1866
175 Fifth Avenue
New York, New York 10010
www.henryholtchildrensbooks.com

Henry Holt® is a registered trademark of Henry Holt and Company, LLC.
Copyright © 2006 by John Himmelman
All rights reserved.
Distributed in Canada by H. B. Fenn and Company Ltd.

Library of Congress Cataloging-in-Publication Data
Himmelman, John.
Chickens to the rescue / John Himmelman.—1st ed.
p.   cm.
Summary: Six days a week the chickens help the
Greenstalk family and their animals recover from mishaps that
occur on the farm, but they need one day to rest.
ISBN-13: 978-0-8050-7951-7
ISBN-10: 0-8050-7951-3
[1. Chickens—Fiction. 2. Farms—Fiction. 3. Domestic animals—Fiction.
4. Days—Fiction. 5. Humorous stories.] I. Title.
PZ7.H5686Chi 2006   [E]—dc22   2005020044

First Edition—2006
Printed in the United States of America on acid-free paper. ∞

1 2 3 4 5 6 7 8 9 10

Black Prisma color pencil for the outlines and watercolor paint
were used to create the illustrations for this book.

For Tina—
how's this?

On Monday, Farmer Greenstalk dropped his watch down the well.

Chickens to the rescue!

"Those are some chickens!" said Farmer Greenstalk.

On Tuesday, Mrs. Greenstalk was too tired to make dinner.

Chickens to the rescue!

"What dear chickens you are," said Mrs. Greenstalk.

On Wednesday, the dog ate Jeffrey Greenstalk's book report that was due the next morning.

Chickens to the rescue!

"Smart chickens," said Jeffrey Greenstalk.

On Thursday, Ernie the duck drove off with the farmer's truck.

Chickens to the rescue!

"Quack," said Ernie.

On Friday, a big wind blew Milky the cow into a tree.

Chickens to the rescue!

"Moo," said Milky.

On Saturday, the sheep wandered off and got lost.

Chickens to the rescue!

"Baa," said the sheep.

On Sunday, Emily Greenstalk spilled
her breakfast all over the floor.

"Um, big mess here, if anyone's listening," she said.

The Greenstalks went out to the chicken coop.

The chickens were fast asleep.

"Sleep well," said Emily.

"You've earned it."